Sharp Judgment

Mastering the Art of Decision-Making

Deepak Singh

ISBN 978-93-5667-736-4
© Deepak Singh 2023

Published in India 2023 by Pencil

A brand of
One Point Six Technologies Pvt. Ltd.
Unit no. 26, Ground Floor, Building A1,
Wadala Truck Terminal Road,
Near Post Office, Antop Hill, Mumbai - 400037
E connect@thepencilapp.com
W www.thepencilapp.com

Author biography

Hello! I'm happy to meet you, I'm Deepak Singh. I work as a research analyst and am passionate about writing books and doing research on the planet Earth, space, and the art of living. I most likely have high analytical and critical thinking abilities that enable me to assess data, spot trends, and reach conclusions in my capacity as a research analyst. As part of my job, I might perform primary and secondary research, analyze available data, and provide findings to guide individual, corporate, or organizational decision-making. I adore writing and researching as interests in space and Earth in my free time. You can tell that I have an open mind and am interested in learning about the world around me.

CONTENTS

Foreword

Making correct and educated decisions is more crucial than ever in today's fast-paced and complex society. Every day, we face an onslaught of decisions that have far-reaching effects on our lives and the lives of those around us. Some actions are minor, while others can have far-reaching consequences.

Making good decisions is a talent that can be learned and improved over time. Critical thinking, emotional intelligence, and a grasp of the biases and other factors that can impact our decisions are all required.

In "Sharp Judgement: Mastering the Art of Accurate Decision-Making," the author offers readers a complete guide to making sound judgments. This book presents a practical framework for making effective judgments, from understanding our biases to acquiring and analyzing information, considering alternative views, and evaluating implications.

This book is an important resource whether you are a business professional, a student, or simply someone who wants to enhance their decision-making skills. It is a well-researched and thought-provoking guide that will encourage you to think more critically about your decisions and assist you in developing the skills necessary to make better decisions.

Anyone who wants to become a more successful and confident decision-maker should read this book.

Preface

Making sound decisions is a key ability that can have a significant impact on our lives. Our choices can influence our success or failure, pleasure or suffering, and general quality of life. Unfortunately, many of us have difficulty making effective decisions, either due to a lack of basic abilities or because we are influenced by biases and other circumstances.

As someone who has spent years studying and analyzing decision-making, I understand how critical it is to make accurate judgments. In "Sharp Judgement: Mastering the Art of Accurate Decision-Making," I share my ideas and knowledge on this critical subject.

The goal of this book is to give readers a thorough guide to making sound decisions. I've also included a slew of real-world examples and case studies to show how these ideas might be put into action.

This book is not a quick fix or a magic recipe for making perfect judgments. Instead, it is a guide to assist readers in developing the skills and mindset required to make better decisions over time. It takes time, practice, and a willingness to learn from mistakes.

I hope that this book inspires readers to think more critically about their options and to develop the skills necessary to make accurate and informed decisions. I also hope it will be a useful resource for anyone looking to enhance their decision-making abilities, whether in their personal or professional lives.

Thank you for spending time reading this book. I hope you will find it useful as you traverse the difficult realm of decision-making.

Acknowledgements

A book is never written alone, and this one is no exception. I am grateful to the numerous individuals and organizations who helped in the preparation of this book.

First and foremost, I'd like to express my gratitude to my family and friends for their continuous encouragement and support during the writing process. Their kindness, patience, and understanding have been priceless.

I'd also like to thank my editor and the entire publishing house team for their professionalism, advice, and competence. Their comments and input have helped to shape this book and make it a better offering.

I'm also grateful to the many researchers and academics who have helped us comprehend decision-making. Their work has influenced my studies and writing.

Finally, I'd like to offer my appreciation to the book's readers. I sincerely hope that this book will be a useful resource for anyone looking to improve their decision-making abilities. Your criticism and comments are always welcome, and I eagerly await your responses.

Introduction

Making sound judgments is a necessary ability that can have a significant impact on our lives. From minor daily decisions to large life-altering decisions, the capacity to make educated and correct judgments can help us achieve our goals, avoid pitfalls, and live better, more satisfying lives.

Despite its importance, many of us struggle to make sound decisions. Biases, emotions, and other circumstances can all cloud our judgment and lead us down the incorrect path. We may also lack the required abilities and instruments to effectively obtain and analyze information, consider alternative perspectives, and assess its implications.

In "Sharp Judgement: Mastering the Art of Accurate Decision-Making," we give readers a step-by-step strategy for making sound decisions. We give practical advice and resources for building the skills and mentality required for effective decision-making, based on the most recent research from psychology, neuroscience, and other domains.

We will look at the key components of good judgment throughout this book, such as critical thinking, emotional intelligence, and an understanding of the biases and other factors that can impact our judgments. We also give readers a practical foundation for making effective decisions, such as advice on acquiring and analyzing information, evaluating options, and contemplating the potential implications of our actions.

This book is an important resource, whether you are a business professional, a student, or simply someone who wants to enhance their decision-making skills. It provides practical advice and decision-making tools, as well as real-world examples and case studies that show how these concepts can be utilized in practice.

We hope that this book inspires readers to think more critically about their decisions and to build the skills and mentality required for accurate and informed decision-making. We also hope that it will be a useful resource for anyone looking to enhance their decision-making abilities, both personally and professionally.

Chapter 1 Recognise Your Biases

Bias Definition and Impact on Decision-making

Biases are systematic flaws in decision-making that can affect our judgment and lead to incorrect or unreasonable decisions. They are a normal element of the human cognitive process, and everyone is vulnerable to them, even if they are not conscious of them.

Biases can be generated by a variety of causes, such as previous experiences, cultural standards, cognitive limits, and personal views. They can influence our decision-making in a variety of ways, from how we interpret information to how we weigh risks and benefits.

Confirmation bias is one of the most common types of bias. This happens when we seek knowledge that validates our existing views while ignoring information that challenges them. For example, if we believe that a specific political candidate is the best choice for office, we may seek out only news stories or viewpoints that support that belief, ignoring any evidence to the contrary. Confirmation bias can cause a distorted picture of reality and impair our ability to make sound judgments.

The availability heuristic is yet another prevalent prejudice. This is the inclination to make decisions based on how easily examples spring to mind. For example, if we hear about a recent crime in our neighborhood, we may mistakenly believe that crime rates are high, even if they are not. The availability heuristic can drive us to overestimate dangers and make judgments based on insufficient or erroneous information.

Another sort of prejudice that can influence our decision-making is anchoring bias. This happens when we make a decision based on the first piece of information we receive. If we are discussing pay with a possible employer and they offer us a low starting point, we may build our expectations on that initial offer, even if it is lower than what we are actually worth. Anchoring bias can impede our capacity to bargain successfully and lead to missed opportunities.

The availability heuristic, confirmation bias, and anchoring bias are just a handful of the many biases that might influence human decision-making. They can lead to erroneous judgments, poor decisions, and missed opportunities. To reduce the influence of biases on our decision-making, we must be conscious of them and actively seek out varied perspectives and facts. As a result, we can make better informed and productive decisions that are less subject to bias.

Common biases and how they influence our decisions

When making decisions, our brains are designed to take shortcuts. These cognitive biases are mental shortcuts that help us make quick decisions based on limited information. While these biases might be useful in some instances, they can also contribute to poor judgment and decision-making. In this chapter, we will look at some of the most frequent cognitive biases and how they influence our decisions.

- **Confirmation Bias:**Confirmation bias is the tendency to seek out information that confirms our pre-existing opinions while ignoring information that contradicts them. For example, if you believe that a particular political party is bad for the economy, you may only seek out news pieces that support that belief and overlook those that contradict it. Confirmation bias can lead to narrow-mindedness and the refusal to examine alternative points of view. It can also make it difficult to change our opinions when confronted with new facts that contradict our beliefs.

- **Availability Bias:**The tendency to make decisions based on easily available information is known as availability bias. This bias can cause us to overestimate the likelihood of uncommon, highly publicized catastrophes, such as airline crashes or terrorist attacks, while underestimating the likelihood of more common, less publicized incidents, such as vehicle accidents. The availability bias might sometimes cause us to base our decisions on anecdotes rather than data. For example, if you hear a narrative of someone who became extremely wealthy by investing in a specific stock, you may be more likely to invest in that stock yourself, even though the facts indicate that it is not a smart investment.

- **Anchoring Bias:**The propensity to rely too heavily on the first piece of information we get while making a decision, even if that information is irrelevant or deceptive, is known as anchoring bias. If you're negotiating the price of a used car, for example, the original asking price might serve as an anchor for your negotiations, even if it's far more than the car's true value. Anchoring bias might cause us to make poor decisions by limiting our possibilities. It can also cause us to overvalue certain pieces of information while undervaluing others that may be more important.

- **Hindsight Bias:**The tendency to believe that we could have foreseen an event or outcome after it has occurred is known as hindsight bias. For example, after a stock market crash, many people may claim that they predicted it, even though they did not. Due to hindsight bias, we may overestimate our capacity to anticipate the future while underestimating the influence of chance in events. It can also lead to us being too judgmental of poor decisions, even if those decisions were justified given the knowledge available at the time.

- **The Bottom Line:**Cognitive biases are a normal element of the decision-making process in the human brain. However, by being aware of these biases and how they might affect our judgments, we can make better decisions and avoid some of the difficulties that come with depending too heavily on mental shortcuts. While cognitive biases might be beneficial in some contexts, they can also lead us astray if we are not cautious. We can make more informed and rational decisions if we remain watchful and evaluate all relevant facts.

Methods for Identifying and Overcoming Biases

Biases are part of human nature and can influence our decision-making. These prejudices, whether conscious or unconscious, might result in unfair treatment of others. It is critical to recognize and overcome biases in order to develop a fair and just society. This chapter will go through ways of identifying and overcoming biases.

- **Recognize your biases:**Recognizing prejudices is the first step towards overcoming them. Be conscious of your personal prejudices and how they may influence your decision-making. Take some time to consider your attitudes and views about various categories of people. This can be a difficult undertaking because many biases are firmly embedded, yet it is necessary for personal growth and development.

- **Seek out diverse perspectives:**Seeking out varied opinions is one of the most effective strategies to overcome biases. Experimenting with diverse cultures, beliefs, and backgrounds can extend your perspective and challenge your ideas. Seek out opportunities to interact with people from other backgrounds, read a variety of books and articles, and participate in open-minded discussions with others.

- **Practice empathy:**The ability to comprehend and share the sentiments of others is referred to as empathy. Empathy training can help us overcome biases by putting ourselves in the shoes of others. This is attempting to perceive the world through their eyes, acknowledging their emotions, and treating them with respect and empathy.

- **Educate yourself:**Education is an extremely effective strategy for eliminating prejudices. Learn about diverse cultures, faiths, and lifestyles. Discover the history and experiences of marginalized groups. This can help you better comprehend and appreciate diversity, as well as identify biases.

- **Challenge stereotypes:**Stereotypes are simplistic and frequently incorrect generalizations about a specific group of people. By questioning preconceptions and seeking facts to support or disprove them, you can challenge them. Avoid stereotypical language and behavior, and encourage others to do the same.

- **Use objective criteria:** When making decisions, it is critical to apply objective criteria to counteract prejudices. This entails paying attention to facts and evidence rather than assumptions and stereotypes. Rather than depending on subjective judgments or personal prejudices, use objective methods to evaluate performance and potential.

- **Take responsibility:**Finally, accept personal accountability for your actions and decisions. Recognize the presence of prejudices and take action to overcome them. If you make a mistake, admit it and work to remedy it. Maintain accountability for your activities and make a commitment to constant self-improvement.

To summarize, biases are an unavoidable aspect of human nature, but they can be overcome with work and understanding. We may develop a more fair and equitable society by recognizing our prejudices, finding out other perspectives, practicing empathy, educating ourselves, fighting stereotypes, utilizing objective standards, and accepting responsibility.

Chapter 2 Obtaining Information

The significance of acquiring accurate and relevant data

Accurate and relevant information is vital for making decisions in practically every aspect of life. Whether you're making a personal or corporate decision, the information you acquire will be critical in determining whether your endeavors succeed or fail. In this chapter, we will look at how important it is to acquire accurate and relevant information and how it might affect the consequences of our judgments.

To begin, accurate and relevant information contributes to a firm foundation for decision-making. It enables us to make informed judgments based on accurate and dependable data. We may make decisions based on assumptions, views, or obsolete knowledge if we lack accurate and relevant information, which can lead to poor decision-making and bad repercussions.

For example, a company that depends on obsolete market research data may make judgments based on incorrect assumptions about client requirements and preferences, resulting in products that do not match market demands. A company that engages in frequent market research to obtain reliable and relevant information about its customers, on the other hand, is more likely to make decisions that result in successful product launches and customer satisfaction.

Second, accurate and relevant information aids in the reduction of uncertainty and risk. Making decisions without appropriate information can be dangerous, as there may be unknown variables or factors that can influence the decision's outcome. Accurate and relevant information aids in the identification and mitigation of risks, making decision-making more predictable and trustworthy.

Before accepting a new job offer, a person may acquire information on the company's financial soundness, work culture, and employee satisfaction. This information can assist them in evaluating the potential risks and rewards of the employment offer, thereby decreasing the ambiguity connected with the decision.

Finally, acquiring accurate and relevant information can assist in identifying areas for growth and improvement. We can discover developing trends, shifting customer preferences, and new market opportunities by gathering information on a regular basis, which can help us make strategic decisions that lead to growth and success.

A company that continuously obtains information about its industry and competitors, for example, may uncover a market gap that it may fill with a new product or service, resulting in higher revenue and market share.

Finally, acquiring correct and relevant information is an important aspect of decision-making. It provides a firm platform for decision-making, minimizes ambiguity and risk, and aids in the identification of growth and improvement prospects. Investing time and money in acquiring reliable and relevant information is critical to attaining your goals and objectives, whether you are making personal or corporate decisions.

Methods for effectively acquiring information

Gathering knowledge is an important skill for success in today's fast-paced society. The ability to gather relevant and reliable information can make or break a school project, a company proposal, or personal research. However, with so much information available on the internet and elsewhere, it can be difficult to navigate through it all and locate what you need. In this chapter, we will look at different strategies for properly acquiring information.

- **Establish Your Goals:**It is critical to clarify your objectives before you begin gathering information. What do you hope to accomplish with the information you collect? What questions must you answer? You can focus your efforts and avoid spending time on useless material by stating your objectives.

- **Make Use of a Variety of Sources:**It's critical to use a range of sources when acquiring knowledge. Do not rely on a single website, book, or person. To gain a more comprehensive understanding of your issue, use a variety of sources. Books, scholarly journals, news articles, blogs, podcasts, interviews, and other materials may be included. The greater the number of sources you employ, the more diverse and balanced your knowledge will be.

- **Examine the Reputability of Your Sources:**Not every source is created equal. Some sources may be biased, incorrect, or out of date. It is critical to assess the credibility of your sources before relying on them. Seek out credible sources such as academic journals, government websites, and well-known news channels. Examine the author's qualifications and affiliations. Cross-check a source's trustworthiness with other sources if you're unsure.

- **Take Notifications:**It is critical to take notes when acquiring information. This aids in remembering what you've learned and organizing your ideas. It also helps to reference your sources later on. There are numerous note-taking techniques available, including outlining, mind mapping, and bullet points. Choose the method that works best for you.

- **Pose Questions:**When obtaining information, don't be scared to ask questions. Asking specialists on the topic, contacting writers of articles or books, or engaging in internet forums are all examples of this. Asking questions can help you clarify ambiguous facts and gain new views on your issue.

- **Utilise Search Operators:**When using search engines like Google, it's critical to employ search operators to narrow down your results. You can use these special commands to filter your results. You can, for example, use quotes to search for a specific phrase, the minus sign to eliminate specific phrases, or the site: operator to search within a specific website.

- **Maintain Order in Your Research:**Finally, it is critical to organize your research. Writing a folder on your computer for your research, utilizing a citation manager to keep track of your sources, or writing an outline to help you structure your results are all examples of this. You may save time and minimize misunderstandings by keeping your research organized.

Finally, properly acquiring information necessitates a combination of abilities and tactics. You can obtain relevant and accurate information that will help you reach your goals by defining your objectives, using a range of sources, evaluating the authenticity of your sources, taking notes, asking questions, using search operators, and keeping your research organized.

How to Assess the Quality of Information

We are continuously assaulted with information from many sources in today's digital world. With so much information available, it's critical to understand how to assess the quality of the material you encounter. Evaluating the quality of information is critical for making educated decisions, avoiding disinformation, and ensuring that the information we receive is credible and trustworthy. Here are some guidelines for determining the quality of information.

- **Examine the source:**The information's source is critical to establishing its reliability. Before accepting information as true, always examine its source. Is it a credible and well-known source? Is it an official government website, an academic institution, or a well-known news organization? If the source is unknown or untrustworthy, it is best to confirm the information from another source.

- **Check out the information:**It's usually a good idea to double-check facts, especially if they appear too good to be true. Examine whether the material is supported by credible sources such as academic journals, government reports, or industry publications. If the information cannot be validated, it is best to proceed with caution or dismiss it entirely.

- **Keep an eye out for bias:**When analyzing information, it is critical to recognize and understand one's own biases. Consider the source's point of view and whether they may have a prejudice or agenda. If the material appears to be biased or one-sided, it may be worthwhile to seek out more sources to obtain a more balanced perspective.

- **Examine the tone and wording:**The information's tone and wording can also convey indicators regarding its reliability. If the language is highly emotional or sensationalized, this could be a warning sign that the material is not objective. Similarly, if the tone is overly negative or favorable, it could indicate that the source has a hidden objective.

- **Look for factual inaccuracies:**Factual inaccuracies are another sign that the information is not reliable. Examine the material for inconsistencies or contradictions, then cross-check it with other sources to ensure its veracity. If the material is based on an assumption or opinion, it should be labeled as such.

- **Think about the date:**The timing of the material is also a crucial consideration when assessing its quality. Is the information current and relevant? Or is it out of date and no longer relevant? Always check the information's date to ensure that it is current and relevant.

To summarize, evaluating information quality is critical for making informed decisions, avoiding disinformation, and ensuring that the information we receive is credible and trustworthy. You can make more informed decisions and avoid being misled by inaccurate or biased information by examining the source, validating the information, looking for bias, assessing the tone and language, checking for factual errors, and considering the date.

Chapter 3 Investigate the Data

How to logically and objectively analyze information

Analyzing material rationally and objectively is an important ability that can assist you in making informed judgments, evaluating arguments, and forming your own ideas. Whether you're studying a topic for a school assignment, analyzing a news item, or making a personal decision, examining information with a rational and objective mentality will help you navigate the sea of information and avoid falling victim to disinformation or propaganda. In this chapter, we will go over various suggestions and approaches for logical and objective information analysis.

Gather information from reliable sources: Gathering information from reliable sources is the first stage in analyzing information rationally and objectively. Reliable sources provide information that is truthful, unbiased, and objective. Peer-reviewed articles, scholarly books, government publications, and respectable news outlets are examples of trustworthy sources. Be wary of biased or agenda-driven sources, such as political blogs, conspiracy theory websites, or social media posts. When analyzing a source, consider the following points:

- Who penned it? What are their credentials and subject matter expertise?

- What is the source's purpose? Is it intended to inform, convince, or sell?

- Is the source founded on facts and evidence, or on views and conjecture?

Determine the primary arguments and claims: After gathering information from credible sources, the following stage is to determine the main arguments and claims. Arguments are the reasoning presented to support a claim, whereas assertions are the fundamental points under discussion. It is critical to identify the premises (the reasons or evidence presented to support the argument) and the conclusion (the main point being argued) while analyzing an argument. When identifying arguments and claims, consider the following questions:

- What is the major topic of contention? What are the grounds offered to support this claim?

- Are the premises supported by credible evidence or by opinions, assumptions, or fallacies?

- Is it necessary to consider any counterarguments or other explanations?

Evaluate the strength of the arguments: Once the key arguments and claims have been identified, the next stage is to evaluate the strength of the arguments. A powerful argument is one that is founded on credible facts, is logically sound, and is free of flaws. Here are some questions to consider when assessing the strength of an argument:

- Is the evidence offered in the argument trustworthy and relevant to the major subject under discussion?

- Are sound reasoning and logical concepts, such as deductive or inductive reasoning, used in the argument?

- Is the argument flawed in any way, such as with ad hominem attacks, straw man arguments, or false dichotomies?

Consider many perspectives:

It is critical to incorporate several perspectives and viewpoints while analyzing materials rationally and objectively. This entails maintaining an open mind and being willing to examine various ideas and arguments. Here are some questions to consider when examining different points of view:

- What are the key points being argued and their counter-arguments or alternate explanations?

- Are there any biases or preconceptions that should be questioned or taken into account?

- What facts or arguments would someone with a different point of view use to defend their point of view?

Draw your own conclusions:

The final phase is to draw your own conclusions after analyzing the facts, evaluating the arguments, and considering many points of view. This entails developing your own viewpoint based on the evidence and arguments offered. It is critical to be upfront about your thought process and to admit any biases or preconceptions that may have influenced your thinking while forming your own conclusions.

To summarize, rational and objective information analysis is a skill that can be learned and practiced. You can make educated decisions and establish your own ideas based on solid reasoning and evidence by acquiring information from credible sources, identifying the main arguments and claims, evaluating the strength of the arguments, considering alternative perspectives, and drawing your own conclusions.

The importance of critical thinking in making sound decisions

Critical thinking is a necessary talent for making sound decisions in both personal and professional situations. It entails analyzing data, evaluating arguments, and making sound decisions based on evidence and logical reasoning. Individuals who lack critical thinking may be prone to biases, fallacies, and other cognitive errors that can lead to incorrect judgments.

The ability to detect and analyze arguments is an important part of critical thinking. This entails evaluating an argument's premises and conclusions to see if they are logical and well-supported. Critical thinkers must also be able to identify and avoid common fallacies, such as ad hominem attacks or appeals to authority, which can undermine the validity of an argument.

The ability to analyze and understand data is another crucial part of critical thinking. This involves the ability to recognize patterns, draw inferences, and identify any biases or confounding factors that may compromise data accuracy. Critical thinkers must also be able to balance the advantages and disadvantages of various sources of information in order to identify which sources are the most reliable.

Critical thinkers must be able to convey their ideas effectively in addition to analyzing information and evaluating arguments. This includes being able to communicate a clear and coherent argument, as well as actively listening to and responding carefully to the opinions of others. In order to improve their arguments and make more accurate judgments, critical thinkers must also be able to recognize and answer any counterarguments to their own perspectives.

Overall, critical thinking is essential for making sound decisions. Individuals can avoid biases, fallacies, and other cognitive errors that can lead to incorrect judgments by using logical reasoning and evidence-based analysis. Individuals can improve their ability to make informed judgments in both their personal and professional lives by honing their critical thinking skills.

Chapter 4 Consider Various Points of View

Why is it vital to examine diverse perspectives?

When making a decision, it is critical to consider diverse perspectives since it allows us to draw better-educated and intelligent conclusions. Taking the time to comprehend different points of view allows us to weigh the pros and cons of each argument and reach a more balanced and accurate decision.

For starters, considering diverse perspectives ensures that vital information is not overlooked. When we limit ourselves to one point of view, we risk missing important facts that could modify our interpretation of the issue. Each viewpoint offers distinct insights, and by considering several perspectives, we can gain a more complete understanding of the situation.

Second, contemplating different points of view allows us to be more compassionate and open-minded. We can build better empathy for others with various experiences and points of view if we recognize that there are different ways of viewing the world. As a result, individuals and groups may be able to communicate and cooperate more effectively.

Third, examining many points of view can help us avoid bias and prejudice. We all have biases and assumptions that might occasionally influence our decisions. We may, however, question our own biases and get a more objective knowledge of the problem by researching alternative perspectives.

Finally, when making a decision, it is critical to examine diverse perspectives. We may ensure that we have all of the necessary knowledge, develop greater empathy and open-mindedness, and avoid biases and prejudices by doing so. Understanding other points of view may require more effort, but it is ultimately the best method to arrive at a fair and balanced judgment.

How to Collect Diverse Points of View

Making a sound decision needs more than just depending on your own viewpoint. Gathering multiple opinions before making a decision might help you obtain a broader grasp of the topic and make a more educated decision. Here are some measures you can take to acquire multiple points of view before making a decision:

- **Identify the stakeholders:**Determine who or what groups will be impacted by the decision you are going to make. Customers, employees, shareholders, suppliers, and other stakeholders may be included.

- **Reach out to the stakeholders:**Once you've identified the stakeholders, contact them to get their thoughts. This could be accomplished through the use of surveys, interviews, or focus groups. You might also solicit feedback and opinions through social media.

- **Listen actively:**It is critical to carefully listen when gathering perspectives. Avoid interrupting or disregarding others' viewpoints by asking open-ended questions. Respect their ideas, even if you don't always agree with them.

- **Consider diverse perspectives:**It is critical to seek out varied viewpoints when gathering perspectives. This could imply finding out viewpoints from people from other backgrounds, ethnicities, or experiences.

- **Seek out experts:**Seek professional viewpoints in addition to getting perspectives from stakeholders. This could be accomplished through speaking with experts in the field, reading publications or reports, or attending conferences or seminars.

- **Analyze the perspectives:**After acquiring several points of view, spend some time analyzing the facts you've obtained. Look for common themes or points of agreement, as well as points of contention. Consider how each viewpoint may affect the decision you are about to make.

- **Make an informed decision:**After you've gathered and analyzed several points of view, use this information to make an informed judgment. Consider the opinions of all stakeholders and analyze the benefits and drawbacks of each choice.

Remember that obtaining diverse viewpoints is a continual process. Maintain an open mind and be willing to change your decision if new information or viewpoints emerge. You will be able to make more educated and effective decisions that will benefit everyone involved.

Strategies for examining and contrasting various points of view

Evaluating and evaluating various points of view is a necessary ability for making informed decisions and reaching sound judgments. However, the procedure can be difficult and involves careful consideration of a number of aspects. Here are some ways to assess and contrast several points of view while making a decision:

- **Consider the source:**Consider the source of each viewpoint, including their reliability, expertise, and prejudice. Evaluating the source's credibility might help you decide whether to give their perspective more or less weight in your evaluation.

- **Identify assumptions:**Each viewpoint is founded on a set of assumptions. Determine whether the assumptions underpinning each perspective are reasonable and rational by identifying and critically evaluating them.

- **Assess the evidence:**Take into account the evidence supporting each viewpoint, including its quality, relevance, and sufficiency. Examine the evidence objectively to see if it supports the viewpoint being offered.

- **Evaluate the logic:**Examine the reasons and logic used to support each viewpoint. Determine whether any logical fallacies or flaws in reasoning weaken the credibility of the perspective being provided.

- **Consider multiple perspectives:**To acquire a more comprehensive grasp of the subject, consider many views on it. Examine each viewpoint carefully and compare them to determine which is the most persuasive.

- **Consider your own biases:**Be mindful of your personal biases and how they may be influencing your appraisal of various points of view. Try to stay neutral and examine all perspectives fairly, including those that differ from your own.

- **Seek out expert opinions:**Seek expert advice on the subject if at all possible. Experts can provide significant insights and assist you in more effectively evaluating the various points of view.

To summarize, considering and contrasting multiple views while making a decision necessitates the thorough evaluation of a variety of aspects. By employing the tactics indicated above, you will be able to make informed decisions and reach sound judgments based on a thorough grasp of the topic at hand.

Chapter 5 Consider the Consequences

The significance of considering the implications of your decisions

The significance of thinking about the repercussions of your decisions cannot be stressed enough. Every decision we make has the potential to impact not only ourselves but also those around us and the entire planet. Before making a decision, we must carefully consider the potential implications of our actions.

One of the primary reasons for considering the repercussions of our decisions is that our choices can have far-reaching ramifications for others. For example, if we make a hurried decision without considering the consequences, we may unwittingly harm someone else or harm crucial connections. This can have long-term implications that are difficult to reverse.

Another reason it is critical to evaluate the repercussions of our decisions is that they can have a big impact on the world at large. Whether we are deciding how to vote in an election or how to dispose of our waste, every action we take has the potential to benefit or harm the earth. We may make choices that are more likely to have a beneficial impact on the world if we take the time to evaluate the potential implications of our decisions.

Finally, considering the outcomes of our decisions is critical because it can help us make better decisions. We can obtain a better knowledge of the situation and make a more informed decision by taking a step back and thinking through the probable outcomes of our choices. This can help us avoid making rash or irrational judgments that we may regret later.

Finally, the significance of considering the implications of our decisions cannot be overstated. We can make choices that are more likely to benefit ourselves and those around us if we take the time to consider the potential implications of our decisions.

How to assess the likely results of various decisions

Making decisions is an essential part of life, and we frequently have to weigh the pros and cons of several options before making a decision. The process of evaluating prospective outcomes entails weighing the expected effects of each action against one another and picking the one that provides the best overall outcome. In this post, we will look at how to examine the probable outcomes of various decisions while making them.

- **Determine the decision that must be made:**The first step in assessing the probable effects of various actions is to identify the decision that must be made. Consider a variety of possibilities before reducing them down to the most viable ones.

- **Determine the consequences of each decision:**The second step is to determine the outcomes of each decision. This entails contemplating the possible outcomes of each decision, both positive and negative. You can compare and contrast the outcomes of each decision by listing them in a table or chart.

- **Determine the probability of each outcome:**The third stage is to assess the probability of each scenario. Some outcomes may be more likely than others, and it is critical to consider this while making a decision. You can evaluate the chance of each result using historical data or statistical analysis.

- **Consider the consequences of each outcome:**The fourth stage is to think about how each consequence will affect you. This entails taking into account not only the possibility of each result but also the extent of its influence. Some outcomes may have a higher influence than others, and it is critical to consider this while making a decision.

- **Consider the trade-offs:**The fifth step is to weigh the trade-offs between various outcomes. This entails balancing the benefits and expenses of each action against one another. A decision matrix can be used to assess the trade-offs between several outcomes.

- **Make a decision:**The final phase is to make a decision based on the evaluation of possible outcomes. Based on your appraisal of the options, their likelihood, impact, and trade-offs, you can choose the decision that provides the best overall outcome.

To summarize, analyzing the probable outcomes of various decisions while making judgments includes recognizing the decision, determining the outcomes of each decision, evaluating the likelihood and influence of each outcome, considering the trade-offs, and making a decision. By following these procedures, you will be able to make informed judgments that will provide the best overall result.

Strategies for assessing the benefits and drawbacks of various choices

When making decisions, it is critical to analyze the potential advantages and disadvantages of each accessible alternative. This can be accomplished by employing a system for analyzing the benefits and drawbacks of various solutions. Here are some techniques to assist you in making a more informed decision:

- **Make a list:**Begin by making a list of all of your alternatives. Then, for each choice, state the advantages and disadvantages. Take into account all aspects of the option, including the short- and long-term effects.

- **Prioritize:**After you've made your list, prioritize each choice depending on the weight of the advantages and disadvantages. Determine which benefits and drawbacks are most important to you and how they compare. This will assist you in determining which choice is best for you.

- **Make use of a scoring system:**Another technique is to give each benefit and con a score based on how essential it is to you. You may then tally up the points to see which option has the most advantages or disadvantages. When picking between numerous solutions with similar merits and cons, this technique can be useful.

- **Seek feedback from others:**Seeking the advice of others might be beneficial at times. You can get opinions on each option from friends, family members, or even specialists. They might be able to bring a fresh perspective or ideas that you hadn't considered.

- **Think about your values:**Personal values can have a significant impact on decision-making. Consider how each option resonates with your beliefs and how it contributes to your overall objectives and aspirations.

- **Examine your choice:**Take some time to think about your decision after you've made it. Consider the results of your decision and whether they meet your expectations. This can help you learn from your decisions and make better ones in the future.

To summarize, assessing the benefits and drawbacks of many options is a crucial component of making educated decisions. You can make better judgments that align with your aims and values if you use these tactics.

Chapter 6 Examine Your Values

The significance of personal values in decision-making

Personal values are important in decision-making because they provide a framework for evaluating options and making decisions that are consistent with one's views, ideals, and objectives. Values are the guiding principles that determine what is important to a person and inform our attitudes, behaviors, and actions.

Personal values have an impact on decision-making in many areas of life, including professional choices, relationships, and even financial decisions. Someone who values integrity, for example, may opt not to compromise their convictions even if it means passing up a great career offer. Similarly, someone who values family may prioritize spending time with family over working long hours.

Personal values provide individuals with a sense of direction and purpose, which helps them make better judgments. They provide a framework for weighing alternatives and trade-offs. Individuals can ensure that their choices are compatible with their views and principles by aligning their decisions with their personal values.

Personal values, on the other hand, can present difficulties in decision-making. When people have opposing ideals, it might be difficult to make decisions that meet all of their principles. A person who values both financial security and creativity, for example, may find it difficult to choose between a solid job that pays well and a more artistic but less lucrative professional route.

Furthermore, personal values can be influenced by cultural and societal standards, significantly complicating decision-making. Individuals may feel compelled to comply with societal expectations, even if those expectations contradict their personal principles.

Individuals should take time to reflect on their views and priorities in order to make better decisions that correspond with their personal values. Individuals might benefit from this meditation by identifying their basic beliefs and developing a clearer sense of direction in decision-making. Individuals can also challenge their beliefs and broaden their understanding of different values and perspectives by seeking out diverse perspectives and engaging in open-minded dialogues.

Finally, personal values are an important aspect of decision-making because they provide a framework for evaluating options and making decisions that are consistent with one's beliefs and ideals. Individuals can make better decisions that correspond with their principles and lead to more fulfilling lives by taking the time to think about personal ideals and seek out diverse opinions.

What are your values, and how do you prioritize them?

Values are beliefs or ideals that we hold dear and value. They are guiding concepts that assist us in making decisions and navigating life. Identifying and prioritizing your values is essential for excellent judgment because it enables you to make judgments that are consistent with your personal views and aims. The following procedures will assist you in identifying and prioritizing your values:

- **Consider your own experiences:**Begin by reflecting on your own experiences and crucial situations. Consider what values were present at those times. For example, if you felt a sense of pride when you assisted someone in need, this could indicate that you appreciate charity.

- **Determine what matters most to you:**Take some time to reflect on what is most important to you in life. What do you hope to accomplish? What type of person do you aspire to be? Make a list of what comes to mind, then identify the values that underpin them. If you want to be a successful business owner, for example, you can prioritize the values of hard work and determination.

- **Consider your existing behavior:**Consider your existing actions and decisions. Are they consistent with your values? If not, why not? Consider whether you can make any changes to better match your activities with your ideals.

- **Set your values in order of importance:**Prioritize your values when you've discovered them. Consider which values matter the most to you and why. You might find it useful to arrange them in descending order of significance.

- **Make decisions based on your values:**Once you've defined and prioritized your values, use them to guide your decision-making. Think about how your choices connect with your values and how they will affect your life and the lives of those around you.

Remember that values can shift over time, and it's fine to reassess and adapt them as needed. Value identification and prioritization are continual processes that necessitate contemplation and self-awareness. This allows you to make decisions that are consistent with your personal views and aspirations, ultimately leading to a more fulfilling existence.

Methods for matching your values with your judgments

Every day, whether consciously or subconsciously, we make decisions about what is right or wrong, good or bad, just or unjust. Our values, which are the ideas or beliefs that we hold dear and influence our behavior and decision-making, are reflected in our judgments.

However, our judgments may not always be consistent with our ideals, resulting in cognitive dissonance and a sensation of inner conflict. This can occur for a variety of reasons, including societal pressure, cognitive biases, or a lack of self-awareness.

We can use the following tactics to ensure that our judgments are consistent with our values:

- **Make your values clear:**The first step is to identify your core values. Take some time to consider what is important to you, what you stand for, and the type of person you want to be. Write down your values and keep them somewhere prominent where you can see them.

- **Develop your self-awareness:**Recognize your own thoughts, feelings, and behaviors. Examine your judgments to see if they are consistent with your values. Pay attention to any internal tensions or discomfort you may be experiencing and try to pinpoint the source.

- **Examine your biases:**We all have unconscious or conscious biases that influence our decisions. Examine your preconceptions, stereotypes, and prejudices to see if they are supported by evidence or simple supposition.

- **Seek out other points of view:**Seek out alternative ideas and opinions to broaden your understanding of various points of view. This can assist you in challenging your own preconceptions and biases and making more informed decisions.

- **Act with honesty:**Make a concerted effort to match your behavior to your principles. Examine your actions and behaviors to see if they are aligned with your beliefs and represent the type of person you want to be.

- **Consider and adjust:**Reflect on your decisions and behaviors on a frequent basis and make changes as appropriate. It is OK to alter your mind or revise your values in response to new information or experiences.

Finally, integrating our values with our judgments is critical for making excellent decisions that are consistent with who we are and what we stand for. We may guarantee that our judgments reflect our values and contribute to our personal growth and well-being by practicing self-awareness, confronting our prejudices, seeking other viewpoints, behaving with integrity, and reflecting and adapting.

Chapter 7 Make the Choice

How to Make the Final Call

Making a final decision can be difficult, especially when it comes to crucial things that might have a huge impact on your life. Whether you're attempting to decide on a job offer, a lover, or a life-altering decision, it's critical to use excellent judgment and make the best option possible.

Here are some measures you can take to make an informed decision:

- **Gather all the relevant information:**To make an informed decision, it is critical to collect all relevant information. Doing research, consulting specialists, getting counsel from trusted friends or family members, or analyzing your personal experiences and insights may be required.

- **Consider all the options:**Before making a final decision, it is critical to explore all available possibilities after acquiring all necessary information. Consider the advantages and drawbacks of each option, as well as the potential implications and how each option corresponds with your goals and values.

- **Clarify your priorities:**Your priorities are critical in decision-making. Make sure you know what your values are, what is most important to you, and what you want to accomplish in the long run. This will assist you in making a decision that is consistent with your goals and values.

- **Seek advice from others:**Don't be reluctant to seek advice from others, especially those with similar experience. Seek out those you trust and respect, and solicit their feedback. You could also seek professional help from a counselor, coach, or mentor.

- **Trust your gut instinct:**When making a decision, your intuition can be a significant asset. If you have a strong feeling about a certain choice, it may be worth giving it further thought, even if it does not necessarily line up with the logical analysis you've performed.

- **Make a decision:**It's time to make a decision after acquiring all of the essential information, considering all of the options, establishing your priorities, seeking counsel, and trusting your gut feeling. Choose the option that best corresponds with your goals and values and feels appropriate for you.

- **Take responsibility for your decision:**Accept responsibility for your decisions once you've made them. Accept that every decision has consequences, both positive and negative, and be ready to deal with them.

To summarize, making a sound decision requires careful consideration, a clear understanding of your beliefs and interests, and seeking guidance from reliable sources. Trusting your instincts and accepting responsibility for your choices are also important parts of the process. Following these steps will help you make a decision that is consistent with your goals and values and will lead to a more fulfilling and happy life.

Considerations while making a decision

Making choices is an essential element of our daily lives. Our lives are full of decisions, from basic ones like what to eat for breakfast to more significant ones like changing occupations. While some decisions are simple, others are more difficult, and making the A proper choice needs sound judgment. In this post, we will go over some of the elements to think about while making a decision and exercising sound judgment

- **Identify the problem:**It is critical to identify the problem you are attempting to tackle before making any decisions. Clarifying the issue will assist you in understanding the scope of the decision you must make and the potential implications.

- **Gather information:**You need as much information as possible to make an informed decision. Collecting pertinent data, views, and experiences can help you better grasp the situation and make an informed conclusion.

- **Weigh the pros and cons:**Weighing the pros and drawbacks is an important component to consider while making a decision. This entails weighing the advantages and disadvantages of each conceivable option in order to make the optimal decision.

- **Analyze the risks:**Every decision involves some level of risk. It is critical to identify and assess the potential risks connected with each choice in order to determine whether they are acceptable. Knowing the dangers will enable you to make a better educated and considered decision.

- **Consider your values:**Your values and beliefs play an important part in decision-making. Consider how each option matches with your personal values and beliefs, as well as how it may impact your long-term ambitions.

- **Seek advice:**When making significant decisions, it might be beneficial to seek advice from others. This could be from friends, relatives, or subject matter specialists. Their advice can assist you in seeing the situation from various angles and drawing a more educated conclusion.

- **Take time to reflect:**Taking a step back and meditating on your decision might sometimes help you make a better one. Allowing yourself time to consider your options and the repercussions can assist you in making a more sensible and informed decision.

To summarize, making a smart decision takes careful study of the situation, acquiring relevant information, balancing the pros and cons, analyzing risks, considering your values, seeking guidance, and reflecting. Following these steps will allow you to make well-informed decisions that are in line with your goals and values.

Techniques for making difficult choices

Making difficult decisions can be difficult, especially when the conclusion has a large impact on our lives or the lives of others. When making these decisions, use good judgment is vital because it ensures that we assess all of the options, consider the repercussions, and choose the best possible course of action. Here are several approaches to making difficult judgments with sound judgment:

- **Gather Information:**It is critical to obtain as much information about the situation as possible before making any decisions. This includes investigating the issue, acquiring pertinent data, getting expert guidance, and consulting with individuals who have dealt with similar problems in the past. The more knowledge you have, the better you will be able to assess your options and draw an educated conclusion.

- **Identify Your Values:**Decisions are heavily influenced by your values and beliefs. When making a decision, it is critical to identify and prioritize your values. For example, if honesty and integrity are important to you, you may pick a path that corresponds with those values, even if it is not the simplest or most popular alternative.

- **Consider the consequences:**Every decision has both positive and bad implications. Consider the possible results of each decision and how they will affect you and those involved. This covers the influence on your relationships, finances, and personal well-being in the short and long term.

- **Use Your Intuition:**Your gut instinct can be a strong decision-making tool at times. Listen to your intuition if you have strong feelings about a particular alternative or a sense of what the best solution is. However, it is critical to balance your intuition with logical thinking and fact-checking.

- **Seek Input from Others:**When making a difficult decision, it can be beneficial to get feedback from others. Seeking advice from trusted friends or family members, talking with specialists, or soliciting comments from individuals who may be affected by your decision are all examples of this. This can present you with new viewpoints and insights that you had not previously considered.

- **Take Time to Reflect:**A hasty judgment can result in regret and bad repercussions. Before making a final decision, it is critical to reflect on your alternatives, assess the advantages and drawbacks, and analyze the probable outcomes. This could entail taking a step back from the situation, taking a break, or seeking solitude to ponder.

To summarize, making tough judgments requires careful examination of all possibilities and their potential repercussions. You can make educated decisions that correspond with your values and goals by acquiring information, defining your values, contemplating the consequences, using your intuition, seeking advice from others, and taking time to think.

Chapter 8 Consider and Learn

The significance of considering your options

Making decisions is an important part of our daily lives, and our capacity to make sound decisions can have a big impact on our overall happiness. Making effective decisions, on the other hand, is not always straightforward, and we are frequently faced with difficult choices when we have little knowledge or competing priorities.

Reflecting on past decisions is one of the most effective strategies to improve our decision-making abilities. Reflection entails taking the time to analyze our decisions, the results that occurred from those decisions, and the reasons for those decisions.

We may learn from our failures and make better decisions in the future by reflecting on our decisions. We can recognize patterns in our decision-making process and determine when we are acting on emotions or prejudices rather than rational cognition. Reflection also assists us in understanding the implications of our actions and accepting responsibility for the outcomes of our decisions.

To exercise good judgment, we must analyze all available information, weigh potential risks and advantages, and make decisions that are consistent with our beliefs and goals. By reflecting on our choices, we can ensure that they are in line with our long-term goals and consistent with our beliefs.

Furthermore, thinking about our choices might boost our self-awareness and emotional intelligence. It assists us in understanding our own strengths and shortcomings as decision-makers and recognizing when we may require extra information or direction.

Finally, it is critical for excellent judgment to reflect on our decisions. It enables us to learn from our mistakes, make better judgments in the future, and make decisions that are consistent with our beliefs and aims. We can become more self-aware and emotionally intelligent by reflecting on our decisions, making us more effective decision-makers in all facets of our lives.

How to Assess the Outcomes of Your Decisions

Forming decisions, addressing problems, and critical thinking all necessitate forming judgments. However, assessing the outcomes of those evaluations in order to determine their utility and correctness is also crucial. Evaluating the outcomes of your judgments is a vital process that allows you to learn from your mistakes, make better decisions in the future, and grow as a decision-maker. Here are some metrics you can use to evaluate the outcomes of your decisions:

- **Establish your criteria:**Before making a decision, you must first determine the criteria that will be used to evaluate the outcomes. Specific, measurable criteria that are relevant to the choice or problem at hand should be used. For example, if you're assessing the success of a company's choice, your criteria could include financial performance, customer happiness, and employee morale.

- **Gather information:**After you've specified your criteria, you'll need to collect data to help you analyze the results. This could contain financial statistics, customer comments, staff surveys, or other pertinent data. To have a thorough knowledge of the consequences, you need to collect both quantitative and qualitative data.

- **Examine the data:**After gathering the data, you must analyze it to establish the outcomes of your judgment. Examine the data for patterns and trends that indicate whether or not your judgment was effective. If the data indicates that your judgment was ineffective, try to figure out why.

- **Consider your decision:**In addition to analyzing the data, you should consider your judgment to see whether you made any errors or biases. Consider whether you had all of the essential information at the time, whether you were impacted by emotions or prejudices, and whether you overlooked any alternate possibilities.

- **Change your approach:**Finally, change your approach to decision-making or problem-solving based on your review. Use the evaluation's findings to make better decisions in the future.

Changing your criteria, enhancing your data collection methods, or shifting your thought process are all examples of this.

Finally, assessing the outcomes of your judgments is an important phase in the decision-making process. You may enhance your decision-making skills and make better judgments in the future by defining your criteria, gathering data, analyzing the evidence, reflecting on your judgment, and altering your approach.

Methods for learning from mistakes and refining your judgment

Making mistakes is an unavoidable aspect of the learning process. While they might be upsetting and disheartening, they also present a vital opportunity for us to enhance our decision-making abilities. The goal is to approach mistakes with a growth mentality, understanding that they are a chance for us to grow and become better rather than a reflection of our worth or ability. Here are some tips for learning from mistakes and refining your judgment:

- **Consider the error:**Take some time to think about what went wrong and why. What factors had a role in the error? What would you do differently? What did you take away from your experience? Be truthful to yourself and accept responsibility for your actions.

- **Request feedback:**Request comments from others, whether a coworker, mentor, or friend. An outside perspective can sometimes bring significant insights that we would not have explored on our own.

- **Examine patterns:**Examine your blunders for patterns. Is there a pattern of conditions or decisions that lead to mistakes? Identifying trends can aid in the development of strategies for avoiding similar errors in the future.

- **Create a strategy:**Once you've identified areas for improvement, make a plan to address them. This could entail learning new skills, getting extra training or mentoring, or creating new processes or procedures to help prevent future errors.

- **Accept failure:**You should not be frightened to fail. Failure is a necessary part of the learning process, and every error provides an opportunity to grow and become better. Accept your errors as a useful learning opportunity rather than a reflection of your ability.

- **Exercise self-compassion:**When you make mistakes, it's critical to be nice and compassionate to yourself. Beating yourself up or obsessing over your mistakes can be counterproductive, potentially leading to additional blunders. Instead, practice self-compassion by acknowledging that mistakes are a normal part of the learning process and that you are making every effort to improve.

To summarize, learning from mistakes and strengthening your judgment abilities necessitate a growth attitude, self-reflection, seeking feedback, analyzing patterns, making a strategy, embracing failure, and practicing self-compassion. You may strengthen your skills, gain better judgment, and eventually achieve more success by viewing failures as opportunities for development and improvement.

Chapter 9 Conclusion

The significance of considering the implications of your decisions

The significance of thinking about the repercussions of your decisions cannot be stressed enough. Every decision we make has the potential to impact not only ourselves but also those around us and the entire planet. Before making a decision, we must carefully consider the potential implications of our actions.

One of the primary reasons for considering the repercussions of our decisions is that our choices can have far-reaching ramifications for others. For example, if we make a hurried decision without considering the consequences, we may unwittingly harm someone else or harm crucial connections. This can have long-term implications that are difficult to reverse.

Another reason it is critical to evaluate the repercussions of our decisions is that they can have a big impact on the world at large. Whether we are deciding how to vote in an election or how to dispose of our waste, every action we take has the potential to benefit or harm the earth. We may make choices that are more likely to have a beneficial impact on the world if we take the time to evaluate the potential implications of our decisions.

Finally, considering the outcomes of our decisions is critical because it can help us make better decisions. We can obtain a better knowledge of the situation and make a more informed decision by taking a step back and thinking through the probable outcomes of our choices. This can help us avoid making rash or irrational judgments that we may regret later.

Finally, the significance of considering the implications of our decisions cannot be overstated. We can make choices that are more likely to benefit ourselves and those around us if we take the time to consider the potential implications of our decisions.

How to assess the likely results of various decisions

Making decisions is an essential part of life, and we frequently have to weigh the pros and cons of several options before making a decision. The process of evaluating prospective outcomes entails weighing the expected effects of each action against one another and picking the one that provides the best overall outcome. In this post, we will look at how to examine the probable outcomes of various decisions while making them.

- **Determine the decision that must be made:**The first step in assessing the probable effects of various actions is to identify the decision that must be made. Consider a variety of possibilities before reducing them down to the most viable ones.

- **Determine the consequences of each decision:**The second step is to determine the outcomes of each decision. This entails contemplating the possible outcomes of each decision, both positive and negative. You can compare and contrast the outcomes of each decision by listing them in a table or chart.

- **Determine the probability of each outcome:**The third stage is to assess the probability of each scenario. Some outcomes may be more likely than others, and it is critical to consider this while making a decision. You can evaluate the chance of each result using historical data or statistical analysis.

- **Consider the consequences of each outcome:**The fourth stage is to think about how each consequence will affect you. This entails taking into account not only the possibility of each result but also the extent of its influence. Some outcomes may have a higher influence than others, and it is critical to consider this while making a decision.

- **Consider the trade-offs:**The fifth step is to weigh the trade-offs between various outcomes. This entails balancing the benefits and expenses of each action against one another. A decision matrix can be used to assess the trade-offs between several outcomes.

- **Make a decision:**The final phase is to make a decision based on the evaluation of possible outcomes. Based on your appraisal of the options, their likelihood, impact, and trade-offs, you can choose the decision that provides the best overall outcome.

To summarize, analyzing the probable outcomes of various decisions while making judgments includes recognizing the decision, determining the outcomes of each decision, evaluating the likelihood and influence of each outcome, considering the trade-offs, and making a decision. By following these procedures, you will be able to make informed judgments that will provide the best overall result.

Strategies for assessing the benefits and drawbacks of various choices

When making decisions, it is critical to analyze the potential advantages and disadvantages of each accessible alternative. This can be accomplished by employing a system for analyzing the benefits and drawbacks of various solutions. Here are some techniques to assist you in making a more informed decision:

- **Make a list:**Begin by making a list of all of your alternatives. Then, for each choice, state the advantages and disadvantages. Take into account all aspects of the option, including the short- and long-term effects.

- **Prioritize:**After you've made your list, prioritize each choice depending on the weight of the advantages and disadvantages. Determine which benefits and drawbacks are most important to you and how they compare. This will assist you in determining which choice is best for you.

- **Make use of a scoring system:**Another technique is to give each benefit and con a score based on how essential it is to you. You may then tally up the points to see which option has the most advantages or disadvantages. When picking between numerous solutions with similar merits and cons, this technique can be useful.

- **Seek feedback from others:**Seeking the advice of others might be beneficial at times. You can get opinions on each option from friends, family members, or even specialists. They might be able to bring a fresh perspective or ideas that you hadn't considered.

- **Think about your values:**Personal values can have a significant impact on decision-making. Consider how each option resonates with your beliefs and how it contributes to your overall objectives and aspirations.

- **Examine your choice:**Take some time to think about your decision after you've made it. Consider the results of your decision and whether they meet your expectations. This can help you learn from your decisions and make better ones in the future.

To summarize, assessing the benefits and drawbacks of many options is a crucial component of making educated decisions. You can make better judgments that align with your aims and values if you use these tactics.

9 789356 677364